To my family. —D. M.

For my son, my sweet little Ricky monster. —T. C. K.

Book design by Karyn Nelson.
Typeset in Blue Type and Pillow Talk.
The illustrations in this book were rendered in color pencil and pastels.

Text copyright © 2000 by Derek Munson.
Illustrations copyright © 2000 by Tara Calahan King.
All rights reserved. Published by Scholastic Inc., 557 Broadway, New York, NY 10012,
by arrangement with Chronicle Books LLC.
Printed in the U.S.A.

ISBN-13: 978-1-338-13275-5
ISBN-10: 1-338-13275-X

12   40   25 24 23 22 21 20

Enemy Pie

by Derek Munson

illustrated by Tara Calahan King

SCHOLASTIC INC.

It should have been a perfect summer. My dad helped me build a tree house in our backyard. My sister was at camp for three whole weeks. And I was on the best baseball team in town. It should have been a perfect summer. But it wasn't.

It was all good until Jeremy Ross moved into the neighborhood, right next door to my best friend Stanley. I did not like Jeremy Ross. He laughed at me when he struck me out in a baseball game. He had a party on his trampoline, and I wasn't even invited. But my best friend Stanley was.

Jeremy Ross was the one and only person on my enemy list. I never even had an enemy list until he moved into the neighborhood. But as soon as he came along, I needed one. I hung it up in my tree house, where Jeremy Ross was not allowed to go.

Dad understood stuff like enemies. He told me that when he was my age, he had enemies, too. But he knew of a way to get rid of them. I asked him to tell me how.

"Tell you how? I'll show you how!" he said. He pulled a really old recipe book off the kitchen shelf. Inside, there was a worn-out scrap of paper with faded writing. Dad held it up and squinted at it.

"Enemy Pie," he said, satisfied.

You may be wondering what exactly is in Enemy Pie. I was wondering, too. But Dad said the recipe was so secret, he couldn't even tell me. I decided it must be magic. I begged him to tell me something—anything.

"I will tell you this," he said. "Enemy Pie is the fastest known way to get rid of enemies."

Now, of course, this got my mind working. What kinds of things—disgusting things—would I put into a pie for an enemy? I brought Dad some weeds from the garden, but he just shook his head. I brought him earthworms and rocks, but he didn't think he'd need those. I gave him the gum I'd been chewing on all morning. He gave it right back to me.

I went out to play, alone. I shot baskets until the ball got stuck on the roof. I threw a boomerang that never came back to me. And all the while, I listened to the sounds of my dad chopping and stirring and blending the ingredients of Enemy Pie. This could be a great summer after all.

Enemy Pie was going to be awful. I tried to imagine how horrible it must smell, or worse yet, what it would look like. But when I was in the backyard, looking for ladybugs, I smelled something really, really, really good. And as far as I could tell, it was coming from our kitchen. I was a bit confused.

I went in to ask Dad what was wrong. Enemy Pie shouldn't smell this good. But Dad was smart. "If Enemy Pie smelled bad, your enemy would never eat it," he said. I could tell he'd made Enemy Pie before.

The buzzer rang, and Dad put on the oven mitts and pulled the pie out of the oven. It looked like plain, old pie. It looked good enough to eat! I was catching on.

But still, I wasn't really sure how this Enemy Pie worked. What exactly did it do to enemies? Maybe it made their hair fall out, or their breath stinky. Maybe it made bullies cry. I asked Dad, but he was no help. He wouldn't tell me a thing.

But while the pie cooled, he filled me in on my job.

He talked quietly. "There is one part of Enemy Pie that I can't do. In order for it to work, you need to spend a day with your enemy. Even worse, you have to be nice to him. It's not easy. But that's the only way that Enemy Pie can work. Are you sure you want to go through with this?"

Of course I was.

It sounded horrible. It was scary. But it was worth a try. All I had to do was spend one day with Jeremy Ross, then he'd be out of my hair for the rest of my life. I rode my bike to his house and knocked on the door.

When Jeremy opened the door, he seemed surprised. He stood on the other side of the screen door and looked at me, waiting for me to say something. I was nervous.

"Can you play?" I asked.

He looked confused. "I'll go ask my mom," he said. He came back with his shoes in his hand. His mom walked around the corner to say hello.

"You boys stay out of trouble," she said, smiling.

We rode bikes for a while and played on the trampoline. Then we made some water balloons and threw them at the neighbor girls, but we missed. Jeremy's mom made us lunch. After lunch we went over to my house.

It was strange, but I was kind of having fun with my enemy. He almost seemed nice. But of course I couldn't tell Dad that, since he had worked so hard to make this Enemy Pie.

Jeremy Ross liked my basketball hoop. He said he wished he had a basketball hoop, but they didn't have room for one. I let him win a game, just to be nice.

Jeremy Ross knew how to throw a boomerang. He threw it and it came right back to him. I threw it and it went over my house and into the backyard. When we climbed over the fence to find it, the first thing Jeremy noticed was my tree house.

My tree house was *my* tree house. I was the boss. If my sister wanted in, I didn't have to let her. If my dad wanted in, I didn't have to let him. And if Jeremy wanted in....

"Can we go in it?" he asked.

I knew he was going to ask me that! But he was the top person, the ONLY person, on my enemy list. And enemies aren't allowed in my tree house.

But he did teach me to throw a boomerang. And he did have me over for lunch. And he did let me play on his trampoline. He wasn't being a very good enemy.

"Okay," I said, "but hold on."

I climbed up ahead of him and tore the enemy list off the wall.

  I had a checkerboard and some cards in the tree house, and we played games until my dad called us down for dinner. We pretended we didn't hear him, and when he came out to get us, we tried to hide from him. But somehow he found us.

Dad made us macaroni and cheese for dinner—my favorite. It was Jeremy's favorite, too! Maybe Jeremy Ross wasn't so bad after all. I was beginning to think that maybe we should just forget about Enemy Pie.

But sure enough, after dinner, Dad brought out the pie. I watched as he cut the pie into eight thick slices.

"Dad," I said, "it sure is nice having a new friend in the neighborhood." I was trying to get his attention and trying to tell him that Jeremy Ross was no longer my enemy. But Dad only smiled and nodded. I think he thought I was just pretending.

Dad dished up three plates, side by side, with big pieces of pie and giant scoops of ice cream. He passed one to me and one to Jeremy.

"Wow!" Jeremy said, looking at the pie, "my dad never makes pies like this."

It was at this point that I panicked. I didn't want Jeremy to eat Enemy Pie! He was my friend! I couldn't let him eat it!

"Jeremy, don't eat it! It's bad pie! I think it's poisonous or something!"
Jeremy's fork stopped before reaching his mouth. He crumpled his
eyebrows and looked at me funny. I felt relieved. I had saved his life. I was
a hero.

"**If** it's so bad," Jeremy asked, "then why has your dad already eaten half of it?" I turned to look at my dad. Sure enough, he was eating Enemy Pie!

"Good stuff," he mumbled through a mouthful. And that was all he said. I sat there watching them eat Enemy Pie for a few seconds. Dad was laughing. Jeremy was happily eating. And neither of them was losing any hair! It seemed safe enough, so I took a tiny taste. Enemy Pie was delicious!

After dessert, Jeremy rode his bike home but not before inviting me over to play on his trampoline in the morning. He said he'd teach me how to flip.

As for Enemy Pie, I still don't know how to make it. I still wonder if enemies really do hate it or if their hair falls out or their breath turns bad. But I don't know if I'll ever get an answer, because I just lost my best enemy.

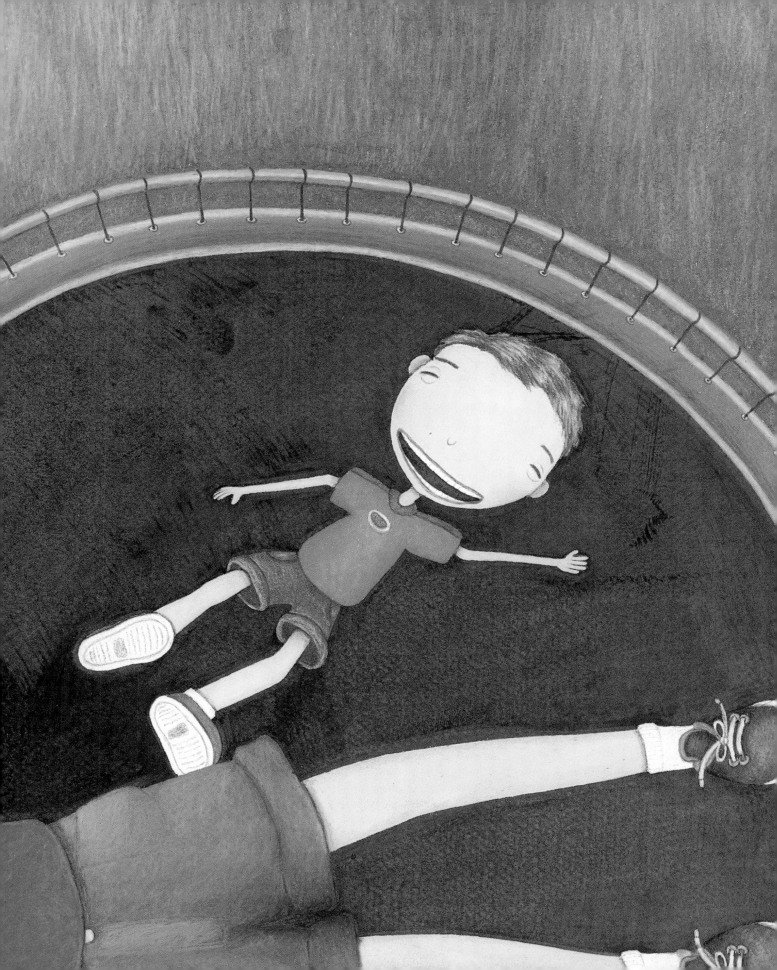